# What Is An Angel?

Illustrations by
Helen M. Salzberg

Adrienne Falzon

Blue Note Books
Cocoa Beach, Florida

www.Bluenotebooks.com

ISBN: 978-0985556228

Library Of Congress Control No.: 2001012345

Cover and Book Design: Paul Maluccio

Original Artwork By Helen M. Salzberg

Printed In The United States Of America

# Dedication

I do believe we are gifted by earth angels as well as heavenly ones. I have been blessed by many earth angels in my lifetime. There are friends, too many to mention, who have genuinely cared for and supported me.

My dear parents Mary and Frank, and Aunt Rose, whose love and guidance were all encompassing.

My four sons, Frank, Paul, Bobby, and Richie, who have given me so much joy and wisdom in the process of life.

My daughter-in-law Erin and grandchildren Olivia and Frankie bring a resurgence of enthusiasm and quest for knowledge.

And, last but certainly not least; this book is dedicated to my husband Manny whose unconditional love and dedication to me can only be the work of an earth angel.

The bell rang...

Olivia looked up at the clock above Miss Quinn's head.

Three o'clock—Time to go home!

Books were slammed shut and papers were noisily shoved into desks.

There was obvious excitement in the air. The children were looking forward to dismissal...and Christmas!

*C*hristmas was only one week away! While Olivia was on her bus line, she looked around her classroom.

There were many pictures of Santa Claus, Christmas trees and cut out snowflakes on the window.

On the wall by the window were the Christmas wish lists of the boys and girls in her class.

However, it was the 3 foot artificial Christmas tree, lit with tiny white lights that attracted Olivia the most.

It stood in the corner, decorated with angel ornaments made by the Art class.

Each angel, hanging gracefully on every branch, was unique since it was created by the imagination of each student.

Olivia looked at her own angel and remembered what she was thinking when she "designed" her angel.

She asked herself again "What is an angel, anyway?"

She decided to ask Aunt Rose when she got home.

Olivia loved Aunt Rose so much. She took care of Olivia when Olivia's mom came home late from work.

When Olivia arrived home after school, she found Aunt Rose in the kitchen, starting dinner and getting Olivia's snack ready.

Olivia knew Aunt Rose would know the answer to her question "What is an angel?"

Aunt Rose knew so many things. She always had wonderful stories to tell about God and how we were made to be happy by loving others.

"Aunt Rose! Tell me! What is an angel?"

"Come here by the table and sit down", Aunt Rose replied, "and I'll try to explain it to you."

Olivia took a bite out of one of the Christmas tree cookies Aunt Rose had just baked.

Her eyes followed Aunt Rose as she sat down beside her.

"Remember, Olivia, how I told you that God loves all of us so very, very much? Well, angels are just another way God loves us.

He gave each of us an angel when we were born. Many people call angels 'guardian angels'."

"The word 'guardian' means 'to take care of' or 'to watch over'.  That is what your guardian angel does for you."

"But, Aunt Rose", Olivia interrupted, "I don't understand. What do they actually do?"

Aunt Rose smiled while she answered.

"They do many things. They are God's Messengers. A messenger is a person who has something to tell us."

"But why do we hang angels on Christmas trees?" Olivia asked.

"Well," Aunt Rose began, "a very long time ago, a special little baby was born.  An angel of the Lord appeared to some shepherds in a field to tell them this good news."

"And, then, all of a sudden, the sky was filled with singing angels.

That day became known as Christmas Day. These were God's messengers at work announcing and celebrating the baby's birth.

We remember those rejoicing angels every Christmas."

"Aunt Rose, how do we know what angels look like?" Olivia asked.

My class drew and cut out angels to hang on our Christmas tree in school and each one is so different! Do they have wings?"

"Well, Olivia, we really don't know," Aunt Rose responded. "The Bible does not tell us what angels look like—only what they do for us. Any pictures of angels that we see that show them with wings, robes, or halos— are just guesses by the artists painting and drawing them."

Aunt Rose looked at Olivia carefully.

"Olivia, it's not important what the angels look like—it's what they do.

Just like I've always told you— it's not what we look like on the outside, it's what we are like on the inside."

"It's how much LOVE we have in our heart for God and everyone we meet.  The more we love, the happier we will be inside of us."

"The angels will lead us to that peace by keeping us surrounded by good people and places. The angels will help us know the right way."

Olivia asked quickly out loud,
"What can I say to my angel?
Can I talk to it?"

"Yes, Olivia, you can talk to your angel any time you want. Ask your angel what to do when you feel sad, sorry, confused, or even angry. We can and must learn from our feelings and problems."

"*O*ur angel will help us see that we are to grow and be a better person with every situation that comes our way."

"Remember, Olivia," Aunt Rose said, quoting a poem:

Our angel is there while you dream
In the endless dark night
She's there while you live
In the broad daylight
Our angel is there when you fail
To show you the way
She's there when you ask
Why me today?

Life has its lessons
In every pain we share
But don't be afraid
Your angel is there

Yes, life has a meaning
And it's all up to you
To open your heart

To learn what is true.

Listen... Love... Be ready
to give
Seek peace in your soul
And you'll be ready to live.

It was a safe feeling knowing she had a guardian angel just for her, sent by God.

What a special gift!

A gift given by God—not only for a Christmas gift or a birthday gift—but a gift for every day of her life.

Olivia remained in her seat, thinking about her new lifetime friend, while Aunt Rose stood up and took the plate of uneaten cookies away.

All of a sudden, the door opened and Mom was home!

Aunt Rose left the kitchen to greet Olivia's mom, and Olivia started to get up to follow, but, before she did, a strange but wonderful soft feeling went across her face...

It was like she was brushed by an angel's wing...